WINCHELL CUTS THE CHEESE

by Taylor Lee and Peter van Dijk

TRICYCLE PRESS

BERKELEY | TORONTO

Tricycle Press
a little division of Ten Speed Press
P.O. Box 7123
Berkeley, California 94707
www.tenspeed.com

Design by Kristine Brogno
Typeset in Minion and Slappy
The illustrations in this book were created by Taylor Lee using
Adobe Illustrator, Adobe Photoshop, and Painter.

Library of Congress Cataloging-in-Publication Data

Lee, Taylor, 1959-
Winchell cuts the cheese / by Taylor Lee and Peter van Dijk.
p. cm.
Summary: A sweet but flatulent pig denies responsibility for the unpleasant odor
detected by the other farmyard animals.
ISBN 1-58246-140-6
[1. Flatulence—Fiction. 2. Pigs—Fiction. 3. Domestic animals—Fiction.]
I. Van Dijk, Peter, 1960- II. Title.
PZ7.L51492Wi 2004
[E]—dc22
2004013154

First Tricycle Press printing, 2005
Printed in Singapore

1 2 3 4 5 6 — 09 08 07 06 05

For our most beloved piglets—
Miranda, Jake, Tia, and Ava

It was early one morning when Winchell woke up.

He stretched his limbs,

then cut the cheese.

"Jeez," said Sheep. "Who cut the cheese!?"

"Not I," said Winchell, sheepishly.

It was later that day when Winchell ate lunch.

He wiped his chin,

"Jimminy Jasper," said Duck. "Who's the Master Blaster?"

"Would you like some fine three-bean salad?"
asked Winchell, ducking the question.

It was early that evening when Winchell went home.

He hung up his hat,

"Whoa, Nellie," said Mutt. "Who cranked that silent but deadly?"

"He who smelt it, dealt it," Winchell muttered.

It was later that night when Winchell turned in.

He brushed his teeth,

"Whoa, Nellie," said Mutt.

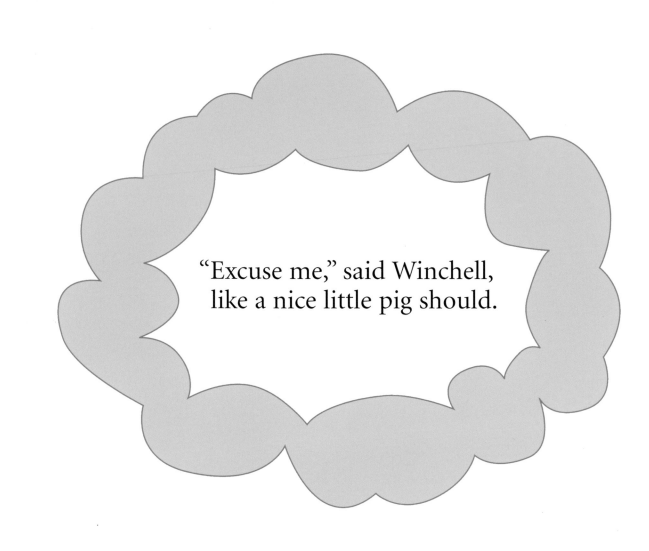

"Excuse me," said Winchell,
like a nice little pig should.

Then he rolled right over

and cut the cheese.

The End